A New F... the Beach

by Michèle Dufresne

Contents

Pioneer Valley Educational Press, Inc.

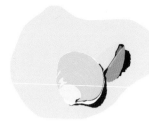

Chapter 1
Olive

It was a sunny morning. Bella and Rosie were at the beach. They were sitting under an umbrella.

"Look!" said Bella.
"Look at that big dog
digging in the sand!"

"Maybe there are bones in the sand," said Bella. "I like bones!"

"Me, too!" said Rosie. "Let's dig for bones!"

Bella and Rosie began to dig in the sand. They made a big hole.

4

"Can you see a bone
in the hole?" asked Bella.

"No," said Rosie.

"Keep on digging,"
Bella told Rosie.

"Look!" said Rosie.
"There is something
in the hole!"

"Is it a bone?" asked Bella.

"No," said Rosie. "It doesn't
look like a bone at all."

The big dog
came over and looked
in Bella and Rosie's hole
in the sand.

"My name is Olive,"
said the dog.

"Hello, Olive," said Rosie.
"My name is Rosie,
and this is Bella."

"Hello," said Bella.

"Did you find a clam?"
asked Olive.

"We are looking
for bones,"
Bella told Olive.
"What is a clam?"

"A clam is a shellfish,"
said Olive.

"What is a shellfish?"
asked Rosie.

"A shellfish is a little animal that lives in a shell," Olive told Rosie. "Look! There is a clam in the shell. Clams are good to eat!"

Bella and Rosie
smelled the clam.

"I like bones better,"
said Bella.

"Me, too!" said Rosie.

Chapter 2
Clam Chowder

Bella and Rosie and Olive walked down the beach. Olive showed Bella and Rosie more clams.

"At the beach you eat clams," said Olive. "And clam chowder."

"Clam chowder? What is clam chowder?" asked Bella.

"Come to my house,"
said Olive.
"You can try
some clam chowder."

Bella and Rosie and Olive
walked down the beach.

They went up the stairs
to Olive's house.

"We will have
some clam chowder,"
Olive said to her
new friends.

"Here are some bowls
of clam chowder,"
said Olive.

Rosie smelled the bowl
of clam chowder.

Bella smelled the bowl
of clam chowder.

"Try it," said Olive.
"It's good!"

Bella tried
the clam chowder.
"It *is* good!" she said.

Bella and Olive ate up the clam chowder.

"I like bones better," said Rosie.

"The clam chowder was good," said Bella.

"I like bones," said Rosie. "Let's dig some more. Maybe we will find some bones!"